Figaro

Excitable and ready for adventure, Figaro knows
the neighbourhood like the back of his paw.

Pixie

Pixie has a nose for trouble
and a very active imagination!

Katsumi

Sleek and sophisticated,
Katsumi is quick to call Kitty
at the first sign of trouble.

For James, Abby, and Megan - P.H.

To my parents who always let me roam free.
And to Murre, the best cat - J.L.

OXFORD
UNIVERSITY PRESS

Great Clarendon Street, Oxford OX2 6DP

Oxford University Press is a department of the University of Oxford.
It furthers the University's objective of excellence in research, scholarship, and
education by publishing worldwide. Oxford is a registered trade mark of Oxford
University Press in the UK and in certain other countries

Text copyright © Paula Harrison 2019
Illustrations copyright © Jenny Løvlie 2019

The moral rights of the author/illustrator have been asserted
Database right Oxford University Press (maker)

First published 2019

British Library Cataloguing in Publication Data

Data available

ISBN: 978-0-19-277165-0

3 5 7 9 10 8 6 4 2

Printed in Great Britain by Bell and Bain Ltd, Glasgow

Paper used in the production of this book is a natural,
recyclable product made from wood grown in sustainable forests.
The manufacturing process conforms to the environmental
regulations of the country of origin.

Kitty

and the
Moonlight Rescue

OXFORD
UNIVERSITY PRESS

Chapter 1

Kitty bounded into her mum and dad's bedroom as gracefully as a cat. She was wearing her stripy pyjamas and her dark hair bobbed around her face as she ran. Flipping head over heels, she landed neatly on the bed.

1

Her mum smiled. 'Slow down,
Kitty! It's nearly bedtime. Aren't you
sleepy yet?'

'No, I'm not tired at all!' Kitty watched her mum take a sleek black superhero outfit out of her wardrobe and put it on.

Kitty's family had a special secret. Her mum had cat-like superpowers and she went out on adventures helping people every night. She could see in the dark, climb walls, and balance perfectly on rooftops. Her superpowered senses meant she could always tell when trouble was near. Best of all, she could talk to cats and share their secrets!

Kitty wished she could be a superhero just like her mum one day. She loved playing rescues in the cat outfit her dad had made her. She could leap all the way from the window seat to her bed without touching the floor.

But when she looked out of the window at bedtime, using her special night vision, there were so many mysterious shadows and odd little noises out there. It was so safe and snuggly in her room and the thought of going out into the dark made her shiver.

She wasn't sure

if she would ever be ready

to be a superhero like her mum.

'Why don't you brush your teeth and

wash your face, Kitty?' suggested Mum.

Her dad came in carrying her little brother.

'It's time for you to brush your teeth too, Max.

Let's find your toothbrush.'

Kitty followed them to the

bathroom, but Max giggled

and scampered away at lightning speed.

Mum caught him and brought him back to the sink. 'Be a good boy and do what your dad says, Max.' She looked in the mirror and straightened her superhero mask. 'It's getting late! I really must go.'

'Can't you read me a bedtime story first?' asked Kitty.

'I'm sorry, honey.' Mum kissed Kitty on the forehead. 'Maybe tomorrow night.'

'I'll read you a story, Kitty,' said Dad.

Kitty's shoulders slumped. She knew

being a superhero was important but she
wished Mum didn't always rush off at
bedtime. 'But I want Mum to tuck me in.
I like our bedtime talks.'

'Why don't we have a little talk now?' Mum took Kitty to her bedroom and they sat on the window seat together.

It was growing dark outside and a bright full moon was rising over the rooftops. An owl hooted in the distance.

'Having superpowers is a very special gift,' said Mum, stroking Kitty's hair. 'On a night like this, when the moon comes out, you can feel magic in the air. Then you know it's the perfect time for an adventure.'

Kitty stared at the darkening sky and gave a shiver. The orange streetlamps were blinking on one by one but strange shadows lingered at each corner. 'But it looks creepy out there. I don't think I could ever be a superhero and go out into the darkness like you.'

Mum hugged her tight. 'You can choose whatever you want to be. But don't let fear hold you back. You're braver than you think!'

Kitty hugged her back. 'I will try to

be brave! I just wish you didn't have
to go.'

'I know, but there are people
out there who might need my help.
Tomorrow we'll have pancakes for
breakfast and I'll tell you all about it.'
Mum smiled and gave her a kiss.
'Sleep tight, darling. Remember, I won't
be far away.'

Kitty smiled back. 'Night, Mum.'
She watched her mum climb out of the
window and run along the rooftop into
the dark.

Dad read Kitty a bedtime story. Then she snuggled down in bed and pulled the blanket up to her chin. Her bed was warm and comfortable, but she didn't feel ready to go to sleep yet. She wriggled on to her side and stared out of the window.

The moon had risen high in the black sky and shadows flickered on the rooftops. The wind whispered outside the window and Kitty's heart beat faster. She turned on her bedside lamp and peeped over the top of her blanket. *There's nothing to be scared of,* she told herself.

Her mum's words spun around inside her head: *Don't let fear hold you back. You're braver than you think!* Maybe she should put on her cat outfit and see if it made her feel any braver?

Jumping out of bed, she pulled her superhero outfit over her head. Then she swung the black silky cape over her shoulders and tied the ribbon carefully. Last of all, she put on her cat tail and velvety cat ears before turning to look in the mirror. She did a perfect spin and the cape flew out behind her. She loved

the way the cat costume looked and she did feel a tiny bit braver.

Suddenly, there was a scratching noise right outside her window. Kitty turned round, her eyes wide. The scratching grew louder and then a shrill meow made her jump. She rushed to the window and peered into the dark.

A sleek black cat with a white face and white paws was waiting on the window ledge. Kitty opened the window and the cat sprang into the room with a flick of his tail.

'Good evening! My name is Figaro.' He smoothed his jet-black whiskers. 'I must speak to

16

your mother at once.'

Kitty gazed at the cat and her heart skipped. Had she really just understood what the cat said? 'Hello, I'm Kitty,' she managed.

'Lovely to meet you!' Figaro gave a theatrical bow. 'Please take me to your mother, Kitty. There's an emergency and I must get her help!'

Kitty's stomach did a somersault. She really had understood him. 'I'm sorry—my mum's already gone out. She left a little while ago.'

Figaro clutched his cheek with one paw. 'This is dreadful . . . but wait!' He stared at Kitty's cat costume. 'You're a superhero too so you can save us from this terrible disaster!'

'Oh, I can't really,' said Kitty. 'I wouldn't know what to do!'

'You are a superhero though,' insisted Figaro. 'Who will help us if you don't?'

Kitty looked
nervously at the thick
black night sky. She'd only been
pretending when she dressed up in
the costume but now this cat believed
she really was a superhero. How could
she tell him that she didn't dare go
out into the dark?

Chapter 2

Kitty looked nervously out
into the night. The thought of venturing
outside made her feel wobbly inside but
how could she explain that to Figaro?
He was expecting her to be a brave
superhero. 'What's happened?' she

asked. 'Is somebody hurt?'

Figaro leapt on to Kitty's bed and flicked his tail impatiently. 'There's an awful noise coming from the clock tower and the animals in the neighbourhood are in great distress!

We have no idea what's making this dreadful racket. You must help!'

Kitty leaned her head out of the window and was amazed to find that her super hearing tuned in at once. The clock tower was a long way from her house, but she could hear a terrible, high-pitched howling. It sent a shiver down her back.

'The clock tower is very tall and the walls are far too slippery for any of us to climb. There is panic out on the rooftops tonight Kitty and we need your help.'

Kitty's stomach lurched. The noise could be anything! Did she really want to go and find out?

Figaro leapt neatly off the bed. He placed his paw on her knee, his face solemn. 'Please Kitty! We really need you.'

Kitty gulped. She really wanted to help and there was also a tiny part of her that wanted to see what it was like to have an adventure. She took a deep breath. 'I'll come to the clock tower if you help me find my way.'

Figaro's whiskers perked up.
'Thank you, Kitty! Every cat in
Hallam City will be forever grateful.'
He skipped to the window, his white
paws flashing. 'Follow me and I'll take
you there at once.'

Kitty put on her orange pumps.
Her heart thumped as she climbed
on to the windowsill. Clouds moved
across to hide the bright full moon and
the darkness thickened. For a second
Kitty nearly turned back inside. Then

she took a deep breath and clambered through the window. She balanced on the roof, her heart racing.

The shadows seemed to stretch out towards her. Stifling a shiver, she gazed around trying to spot places that she knew. There, on the corner, was Mr Harvey's shop with all the cards and magazines in the window. Beyond that was the park with its tall trees and duck pond. The clock tower looked very small in the distance.

The wind stirred and touched the

back of Kitty's neck like a cold finger. A creature with wide wings swooped past with a terrible shriek. Kitty froze—her breath stuck in her throat.

'Don't worry, it's only a screech owl,' said Figaro, bounding away across the rooftop.

Kitty couldn't move. She clutched the chimney pot and the bricks felt rough under her hand. She was just about to tell Figaro the truth—she wasn't really a superhero—when the moon broke from behind the clouds.

Moonlight poured over the rooftop, turning everywhere soft and silver. Kitty suddenly felt her magical superpowers tingling inside from her head right down to her toes! She narrowed her eyes and tuned in her night-time vision. Then she listened carefully and found

she could hear lots of tiny night-time
sounds, from insects chirping to the
whispering of the wind in the trees.

Kitty let go of the chimney and
felt her super balance kick in. It felt
amazing! She skipped across the
rooftop, light as a moonbeam.

'Come on—this way!' called Figaro, leaping from one roof to the next.

Kitty jumped across easily. Then she tried a somersault and landed on her toes. Figaro looked back and nodded approvingly. Kitty smiled at him.

The wind shifted direction and the
terrible howling from the clock tower
grew louder.

Figaro shook his head. 'It's getting
worse. We have to hurry!'

They ran along the next rooftop.
Then Figaro stopped suddenly,
scratching his ear. 'This is no good!
That's much too far to jump.'

Kitty edged on to a narrow
windowsill. 'I think I can see a way
across.' She climbed up the guttering
and ran past a row of chimney pots.

A strange shape moved on the opposite roof. Kitty swallowed. It looked just like a monster with two heads. *It's just a shadow,* she told herself. *Remember: you're braver than you think!* When she looked again she realized it was just the shadow of an oddly-shaped tree.

She bent her knees as she got ready to jump to the opposite roof.

'Help me!' called a little voice. 'Somebody please help me!'

Kitty zoomed in on the sound with her super hearing. 'Wait, Figaro!

Someone's in trouble. I think it's coming from the park.' She clambered down the drainpipe and ran to the park gate.

'Dear, dear!' Figaro puffed a little as he reached the ground. 'What a terrible night we're having!'

Leaving the city streets behind, Kitty and Figaro raced along the winding path that led through the park. The darkness wrapped around them like a blanket and there was a crackling in the undergrowth. Kitty swallowed. It was so dark away from the streetlights and the houses.

The path forked into two. Kitty hesitated, listening again for the cry.

'I'll search this way.' Figaro waved a paw before disappearing in the direction of the pond.

Kitty took the other path, her night vision sharpening. As she dashed around a bend, she spotted a flash of orange fur. A fox with a white-tipped tail lurked at the bottom of a tree. It glanced at Kitty and raised its black nose to sniff the air. Kitty backed away a little. The fox had a sharp glint in its eyes.

'Help me!' called a tiny voice from the branches above.

Kitty's heart raced. Someone was trapped up there! She ran forwards and the fox dashed away, its white-tipped tail flashing in the moonlight.

Kitty peered up into the dark web of leaves. 'It's all right! I've come to help you.'

There was no answer. Hairs prickled on the back of Kitty's neck.

'My name's Kitty,' she tried again. 'Are you OK?'

The silence thickened.

A fluttery feeling grew in Kitty's chest. Even superpowered sight wouldn't let her see through the wild tangle of leaves. Who was up there and why wouldn't they speak to her?

Suddenly, the whole park seemed to be alive with rustlings and whisperings. Kitty gulped. There was only one way to discover who had been calling for help. Finding a foothold in the dark, she pulled herself on to the lowest tree branch and began to climb.

Chapter 3

Kitty swung herself from
one branch to the next and the leaves
above her rustled wildly. As quick as
she climbed, someone or something was
climbing away from her.

'Wait! I came to help you,' called Kitty.

The rustling stopped and a pair of green eyes blinked over the edge of a thick branch. 'Are you sure you're not a monster?' said a little voice.

Kitty realized she had to be talking to a cat. 'I promise I'm not a monster. I'm just a girl but I can talk to cats. It's a special talent that runs in my family,' she explained. 'If you come down I won't hurt you.'

'Oh!' The green eyes blinked again. 'My name's Pixie.' The leaves shook and a small cat with fluffy white fur clambered on to Kitty's branch.

'What happened? Did the fox scare
you?' asked Kitty.

'I was up here in the tree imagining
that I was a magical cat with wings.
Then that horrible howling started.
Can you hear it? I think it's a gh…gh…
ghost!' Pixie's whiskers trembled.

'Figaro says it's coming from the clock tower. I'm on my way to investigate right now,' said Kitty.

Pixie clutched Kitty's arm with her paw. 'You mustn't! What if the ghost sees you?'

Kitty swallowed. 'I'm sure it can't be a ghost,' she said firmly. 'Why don't you come with us and you can see for yourself? The fox has gone so it's quite safe to climb down.'

Pixie followed Kitty down the tree, still muttering about ghosts and monsters. Kitty was starting to wonder if the little cat had a very strong imagination. They scrambled through the bushes, to find Figaro scampering towards them. At his side was a tabby cat with serious, amber eyes.

'There you are, Kitty!' Figaro twirled his whiskers. 'I was getting so worried! Pixie what on earth are you doing here?'

'I was up a tree dreaming of becoming a cat with wings! But now Kitty says I have to come and look at the clock tower ghost,' replied Pixie.

Figaro tutted. 'Dear me! I see you're full of wild ideas like usual.' He waved to the cat with the amber eyes. 'Kitty, I'd like you to meet my friend, Katsumi. She's brought some news about the clock tower emergency.'

'Pleased to meet you.'

The tabby cat bowed her head. She had a beautiful honey-coloured coat and a long, elegant tail.

'Hello Katsumi!' Pixie bounced up to the tabby cat and they touched noses.

'Katsumi, this is my new friend, Kitty,' said Figaro. 'She has special superpowers just like her mother so I asked her to help us.'

Kitty's stomach lurched. 'I'm not really a proper superhero…'

'Of course you are!' Figaro

interrupted, turning to Katsumi. 'Well, what news from the clock tower?'

'An owl friend told me there's a creature on the tower,' explained Katsumi. 'He didn't get close enough to see what it was, but he seemed quite shaken. The noise was overwhelming!'

Kitty listened. She didn't need super senses to detect the sound coming from the clock tower any more. The wailing noise was growing louder and sharper.

'I know a short cut,' said Katsumi

breathlessly. 'Follow me.'

Kitty and the others followed
Katsumi across the park. It was strange
seeing the place at night. Moonlight
glinted on the swings and the slide, and
the duck pond shone like a silver coin.

Leaves crackled and a little owl
with white-and-brown feathers flew
down to perch on the branch of a tree.
Katsumi nodded to the bird. The owl
hooted before spreading its wings and
flying away into the dark.

Leaving the park, they passed a row of shops. Figaro stopped outside a fishmongers and licked his lips. 'Goodness me! That haddock looks delicious.' His stomach gave a deep rumble.

Just then the crying from the clock tower rose into a sharp wail. The noise was so sad and lonely that it made Kitty's heart ache. 'Quickly!' she called to the cats. 'We're nearly there.' She raced down a little alley that took her into a small square surrounded by houses.

The clock tower
was right in front of her,
pointing into the clouds.
The huge clock face was
as round and pale as the
full moon hanging in
the sky. The hands on
the clock pointed at five
minutes to midnight.

Kitty's night vision grew stronger as she stared at the tower's smooth stone walls. She honed in on the terrible noise and spotted a tiny ball huddled on a narrow ledge. It wasn't a ghost or a terrifying monster. It was a little ginger kitten. Its tail was curled around its body and its blue eyes were wide with fright.'

'There's a kitten on a ledge close to the top of the tower,' Kitty told the others. 'I don't know how he got so high.'

'Goodness me!' said Figaro. 'How can one little kitten make such a terrible racket?'

'It doesn't even sound like a kitten,' said Pixie, swishing her silky tail.

'There's a way on to the roof over here.' Katsumi pointed to a house with a low porch. 'Go on Kitty, there's no time to lose.'

Kitty nodded, grateful for Katsumi's sensible ideas. She climbed on to the porch and from there to the rooftop. The others followed her. The

kitten looked down, shivering wildly.
He had soft ginger fur with black stripes
like a tiger cub.

The huge clock face below the
kitten showed the time: four minutes to
twelve o'clock.

Kitty took a sharp breath. Soon it
would be midnight and the clock would
make twelve deafening chimes. The
noise was bound to startle the kitten.
What if it surprised him so much that
he fell right off the ledge? 'Don't be
frightened!' she called to the little cat.

'I'm Kitty and this is Figaro, Pixie, and Katsumi. We've come to help you.'

The kitten stared down at them.

'YOOOWL!' he cried and tears dripped down his furry cheeks.

'Poor thing!' said Katsumi. 'I wonder how he got stuck.'

'He's very young to climb all the way to that ledge.' Figaro shook his head. 'Kittens these days can be so reckless!'

Pixie turned her green eyes to Kitty. 'You will help him, won't you?'

Kitty's stomach felt wobbly. 'I want to try!' she stammered. 'But I'm not really a superhero, I've never actually been on an adventure before.'

'But you were wearing your

superhero outfit!' exclaimed Figaro.

'It's just for playing!' said Kitty desperately. 'I'm really not sure I can do this.'

'You've already come this far,' said Katsumi. 'And superpowers clearly run in your family.'

Figaro frowned. 'Yes! Just remember how courageously you dashed into the pitch-black park when you heard Pixie's cry for help. I thought to myself at the time how brave you were!'

Pixie nodded eagerly. 'I could have been up that tree all night if it wasn't for you.'

Kitty blushed at their kind words. She thought again of what her mum had said: *You're braver than you think.* She turned to face the huge tower and her head spun at the thought of climbing up so high. Then she looked at the tiny ginger kitten, scrabbling at the side of the ledge.

Kitty closed her eyes and felt her powers tingling inside her. 'That kitten's in terrible danger. I know I have to do something!'

A steep drop stretched out in front of her with a narrow stone ledge on the other side. Deep shadows filled the chasm and the cold wind ruffled Kitty's hair. She took a gulping breath. Then she sprang across, landing neatly on the other side. Gripping the stone wall with her fingertips, she began to climb.

Chapter 4

Kitty climbed the clock

tower swiftly, digging her fingers into

the gaps between the smooth stones.

'You can do it!' Pixie cried.

The steep drop below was filled

with darkness, but moonlight poured

over the tower turning the stones silver.
Kitty felt her superpowers rushing
through her and her heart skipped.
Maybe she was a superhero like her
mum after all!

Pulling herself on to the next ledge,
she stopped for a second to get her
breath back. The ginger kitten peered
down with big, wide eyes. There was
a sudden click as the big hand on the
clock moved closer to twelve and the
kitten jumped with fright. Kitty's chest
tightened. It was such a long way down.

She climbed faster, her arms and legs tingling. She could hear the ticking of the clockwork inside the tower. With a loud click, the big hand shifted to point straight at the number twelve. It was midnight!

'Don't be scared!' called Kitty. 'The clock is about to chime.'

The little cat shook as he gripped the ledge. 'What's a chime?'

Bong! The clock made a deep sound. It was so loud that the whole tower trembled. Kitty clung on tightly.

The little ginger cat jumped
in fright then toppled backwards,
tumbling down the clock face with a
terrified mew.

'No!' Kitty shouted.

The little kitten clutched at the clock's long hand and clung to it desperately.

The hand slid back to point at the number eleven. The ginger kitten hung there. He wailed while his little legs swung wildly in mid-air.

'Don't let go! I'll come to get you.' Kitty's powers tingled inside her and she climbed faster than ever. She had to reach the little kitten in time! Nothing else mattered.

The clock carried on striking as

Kitty scrambled downwards . . . ten, eleven, twelve. Just as the last chime rang out, a strong gust of wind swirled around the tower. It made the ginger kitten sway wildly and he lost his grip with one paw.

Kitty's heart pounded. She couldn't let the kitten fall!

'We believe in you, Kitty!' Figaro called from below.

'Go on, Kitty!' Katsumi called out. 'You can do it.'

Pixie leapt up and down, one paw

over her mouth.

Kitty pulled herself on to the ledge below the clock face. The ginger kitten was still dangling from the clock hand and there was no easy way to reach him. Kitty took a deep breath and climbed on to the clock face. She reached out for the closest number, her black cape billowing out in the wind.

Using her superpowers to balance, she clambered from one number to the next. She steadied herself. She was just below the ginger kitten and his back paws dangled above her head.

'I'm here to rescue you!' she told him. 'Reach down and take my hand.'

The kitten's legs wobbled. 'I can't! I'm stuck!'

'Let me help you!' said Kitty. 'You've been so brave hanging on up here. I promise I won't let you fall.'

The little cat gazed at Kitty with terrified blue eyes. 'I really can't move!'

'Be brave!' urged Kitty. 'I know you can do it.'

The kitten's whiskers quivered and he reached down, letting Kitty grab hold of his paw. The little cat let go of the clock hand and Kitty caught him and held him close. She could feel his little body shaking in her arms. The wind swirled around them and Kitty held tight to the clock face. There was still a long way to go until they reached the safety of the rooftop.

'Hold on to my shoulders,' Kitty told the little cat. 'Then I'll have my hands free to climb.'

The kitten
scrambled on to her
shoulders. Kitty made
her way down the
clock face, careful to
keep her balance. The
kitten held tight to
her neck as he peered
anxiously at the
ground.

'It's too far!' he
squeaked. 'We'll never
make it.'

71

'We will,' Kitty told him. 'Can you see my friends on that rooftop over there? Soon you'll be able to meet them.'

The kitten gazed at the rooftop, his whiskers twitching. Kitty went on climbing but the kitten clutched at her face, covering her eyes with his paws.

Kitty didn't want to worry him, so instead she used her superpowered senses. She felt along the tower wall for every foothold and handhold, balancing perfectly. She could hear Figaro and

Katsumi talking on the rooftop nearby so she knew exactly where she was going. At last they reached the wide ledge where she had begun her climb.

'Are you ready?' Kitty asked the ginger cat. 'I'm going to jump across.'

'You mean—all the way over there?' squeaked the kitten, staring at the gap between the clock tower and the rooftop. 'It's too far, we'll both fall!'

'Don't worry, I've done this before.' Kitty smiled. 'And I have superpowers that help me.'

The kitten's eyes turned big and round. 'Then you're a real superhero?'

'I'm still learning,' said Kitty, 'And this is my very first adventure!'

The little cat gazed at her solemnly. 'I trust you! I will hold tight while you jump.'

Kitty got ready, bending her knees and throwing back her arms. Then she made an enormous leap. Her black cape swirled out behind her and for a moment, Kitty felt as though she was flying through the sky. She landed softly on the other side and set the ginger cat down on the rooftop. Figaro, Katsumi, and Pixie rushed over to meet them, mewing with excitement.

'That was such a daring rescue!' gasped Pixie. 'Were you scared, Kitty?'

'A little bit,' Kitty admitted. 'But I knew you all believed in me and that helped a lot.'

'You certainly have great climbing skills,' said Katsumi. 'Don't you agree, Figaro?'

'Yes, indeed!' Figaro twirled his whiskers. 'But I do think it was very silly of this kitten to be up so high in the first place.' He turned to the ginger kitten. 'What in paw's name were you doing up there?'

The little cat's nose twitched and a tear rolled down his furry cheek. 'I was searching for somewhere warm to sleep. I thought if I climbed up high it would be easier to look. Then I realized I was too high and I couldn't get down.'

Kitty crouched down beside him. 'Please, don't cry! What's your name? Do you have any family or friends nearby that can look after you?'

The little cat shook his head. 'I don't have any family or friends at all. I don't have a name either.'

Kitty gazed at him in surprise. How could this lovely kitten not even have a name? 'Well, you have some friends now!' She looked at the other cats and they nodded in agreement. 'We'd love to be your friends if you'd like that too.'

The little cat wiped his tear away with his paw and a slow smile spread across his face. 'I'd like that more than anything in the world!'

Chapter

5

Kitty sat down on the rooftop next to the little ginger kitten. The streets below were dark and silent. Stars glittered overhead like diamonds scattered across the sky.

'So where do you usually like to

sleep?' she asked him.

'I like to find somewhere warm and bright. The thing is . . . ' The kitten twitched his ears shyly. 'I'm a little bit scared of the dark.'

'I sometimes feel like that too, especially when the clouds cover up the moon and there are lots of shadows.' Kitty looked from her friends to the beautiful night sky. She smiled, remembering what her mum had told her. 'But the night time isn't as frightening as I thought. When the moon comes out, you really can

feel magic in the air.'

The kitten nodded, his blue eyes wide.

'Where will you go now?' Figaro asked the

kitten. 'I'm afraid my humans won't let me

bring visitors into our home. I tried it once and

it caused such a kerfuffle!'

The kitten's shoulders drooped.

'I don't really know. Sometimes

I sleep outside the

fishmonger and the shopkeeper gives me a few mouthfuls of fish when the shop opens in the morning, but their doorstep is very cold and hard.'

'You must come with me!' said Kitty firmly. 'Everyone in my family loves cats. You can sleep in my room and I'll make you a delicious breakfast in the morning.'

The ginger cat perked up. 'Really? I can come with you?'

Kitty smiled. 'Of course you can! And tomorrow you can meet my family.'

The kitten frisked up and down with happiness. 'I've always wanted to see inside a real home. Thank you, Kitty!'

Kitty led the cats down from the rooftop and back through the square. When they reached the park, the ginger kitten began to tremble. He yowled at a spiky bush and jumped into Kitty's arms.

'What's wrong?' asked Kitty.

'Nasty spiky thing—looks like a monster!' squeaked the kitten.

'Don't worry—it's nothing to be scared of.' Kitty set him down, but a moment later he jumped back into her arms when a tree branch moved in the wind.

Kitty carried him through the park and he yowled at the park gate, the pond, and the swings. At last his head

began to droop. He
gave one final squeaky mew
at a park bench before closing his
eyes. His stripy head rested on Kitty's
shoulder.

'Poor thing!' whispered Pixie. 'It must be awful finding everything so scary.'

Figaro rolled his eyes. 'Things are certainly quieter now he's asleep. For goodness sake, don't wake him up again!'

Kitty and her friends hurried out of the park and climbed back to the rooftops. They darted along, skipping neatly round the chimney pots. At last, Kitty spotted her bedroom window at the end of a row of houses. She had left her lamp on and it glowed behind the curtains.

'Thank you for helping me with my very first adventure,' she said to Figaro, Katsumi, and Pixie.

'It was our pleasure,' said Katsumi with a bow.

'You did a fantastic job! I expect now you'll want to go on more adventures,' said Figaro, with a wink.

'I expect I will!' said Kitty, laughing.

The ginger kitten woke up and waved his paw sleepily. 'Goodbye everyone and thank you!'

'Goodbye! See you again soon.' Pixie swished her tail happily.

Kitty watched Figaro, with his handsome black coat and white paws, scamper away across the rooftops.

Katsumi followed him, her honey-coloured fur looking pale in the moonlight. Pixie came last, her bright white fur gleaming in the darkness.

Kitty sighed happily. It really had been an amazing night!

She set the ginger kitten down on the windowsill and climbed into her bedroom. 'I hope you like my room. I have lots of comfy pillows and cushions. Would you like to come and see?'

The kitten's whiskers shook. 'I . . . I don't really know! I thought I wanted

to see a real home but . . . what if
I get trapped inside?'

'You won't! And I promise I'll look after you,' said Kitty, surprised.

The ginger cat backed away to the corner of the windowsill. 'I can't go in! Please don't be cross!'

'Don't worry—I'm not cross!' Kitty reached out and stroked the cat between his ears. 'I just don't want you to be cold.'

'I'm quite warm here.' The kitten lay down on the windowsill and curled his tail around his body.

Kitty fetched some cushions and

pillows and brought them over
to the window seat. She left the
window open and settled down on
the wide seat so that she could be
close to the kitten. She could see
his stripy tummy rising and falling
peacefully as he slept.

Kitty hoped he was having
happy dreams. At last she closed
her eyes too and the stars twinkled
above them in the velvet-black sky.

Chapter

6

When Kitty woke up the
next morning, her mum was stroking
the hair out of her face. She sat bolt
upright, puzzled to find herself on
the window seat and not in bed. Then
she remembered everything that had

happened the night before. She peeped
through the open window but the
kitten wasn't asleep on the sill any
more.

'Morning, Kitty!' said Mum. 'You
look like you had an adventure last
night.'

Kitty glanced down at her superhero outfit. 'It was amazing! A cat called Figaro came here looking for you. It was an emergency so I went to help instead.'

'Shall I make us some breakfast and then you can tell me all about it?' said Mum.

'Ooh, yes please! But…' Kitty peered outside, frowning. 'Can you see a little ginger kitten? When I went to sleep he was right here on the windowsill.'

Throwing off her blanket, she leaned out of the window and listened carefully. All she could hear were birds chirping and cars driving along the street below. Kitty's heart sank. She'd wanted to look after the ginger kitten because he had no home of his own. She wished he'd been brave enough to come inside.

'Maybe he's still nearby,' said Mum. 'Why don't you try going outside and calling him?'

Kitty slipped out of the window

and climbed to the rooftop. The sun
shone down warmly and little wisps of
cloud hung in the pale blue sky. Kitty
stopped on the ridge of the roof, calling,
'Hello, are you still here?'

At first, there was
no answer. Then a small
stripy face with whiskers
peeped out from
behind a
chimney pot.
His eyes lit up
when he saw Kitty.

Then he drew back nervously.

Mum, who had followed Kitty, whispered, 'Is he quite a shy cat?'

'I think he's nervous because he's been living all alone until now,' explained Kitty. 'He didn't want to come inside last night. He's not used to having a home.'

'I see!' Mum frowned thoughtfully. 'Well, if he won't come to us maybe we should go to him. Come and help me with the breakfast things, Kitty.'

Kitty and her mum made a stack of

golden pancakes that smelt so delicious they made Kitty's mouth water. They carried the pancakes out to the rooftop along with some fresh orange juice. They also brought out some fresh fish in case the kitten was hungry. They

spread out Kitty's blanket on a small flat area of the roof near the chimney pot.

Kitty poured some honey on her pancake and took a bite. 'Mm! Everything tastes even nicer when you eat outside.'

'It really does!' said her mum, laughing.

'I wonder if this fish tastes good too,' said Kitty, glancing at the chimney pot.

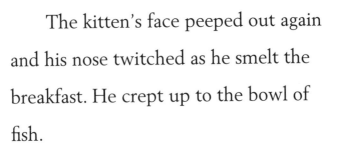

The kitten's face peeped out again and his nose twitched as he smelt the breakfast. He crept up to the bowl of fish.

'Good morning!' Kitty beamed. 'I hope you're hungry.'

'Good morning.' The ginger kitten flicked his tail shyly and then nibbled some food from the bowl. 'This fish is so yummy!'

'Did someone say fish?' Figaro leapt along the rooftop, stopping to preen his sleek black-and-white fur. 'I

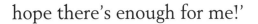

hope there's enough for me!'

Katsumi, who was following, waved her elegant tail. 'Honestly, Figaro! You shouldn't invite yourself to someone else's meal.'

Pixie, who came last, sniffed the air. The sun gleamed on her silky white coat. 'It does smell delicious though. I can imagine I've walked into a splendid banquet!'

Katsumi bowed to Kitty and her mum. 'Sorry for interrupting your breakfast! We just came to say good morning and to thank Kitty for her help last night.'

'Good morning!' Mum smiled. 'You're welcome to join us. I have plenty more fish in the fridge.'

'That is most kind!' exclaimed Figaro while Katsumi and Pixie murmured their thanks.

Mum climbed inside and re-appeared with three extra bowls of food.

The ginger kitten finished his breakfast and licked the bowl with his little pink tongue. 'That was delicious!' He crept over to Kitty and curled up in her lap.

Kitty smiled and stroked his fur gently.

'Good morning!' Dad lifted Max on to the rooftop. 'Do I smell pancakes?'

Soon everyone was eating breakfast and talking about Kitty's adventure the night before. Figaro reminded them all that it had been his idea to fetch Kitty in the first place.

'I was certain Kitty's cat-like superpowers would be just what we needed,' he told everyone.

Kitty blushed. 'I didn't think I could do it . . . but it got easier the more I tried!'

'I'm very proud of you, Kitty.' Mum beamed at her, before turning to the ginger kitten. 'And maybe you'd like to come and live with us? We have plenty of room here and we'd love you to stay. I'm sure it would be nicer than sleeping outside on some doorstep.'

Kitty's heart skipped. She'd hoped her family would love the little ginger cat as much as she did. She held her breath, waiting for the kitten to reply.

'You really want me to stay?' The ginger cat looked from Mum to Kitty. 'Not just for one day but forever?'

'Yes, please do!' Kitty stroked

him between the ears. 'And I think we should help you to choose a name.' She wrinkled her forehead, trying to think. 'How about Pumpkin? It suits you because you have such lovely orange fur.'

The kitten purred. 'I love that name! Do you really think it suits me?'

'It's perfect for you!' Katsumi told him.

Pumpkin rubbed his face against Kitty's and she held him tight, feeling his soft fur against her cheek.

'I think . . . maybe one day soon . . . I'd like to go on another adventure in the moonlight,' said Pumpkin.

'Are you sure you wouldn't be too scared of the dark?' asked Kitty.

Pumpkin thought hard about this.

'Maybe a little bit, but it's much easier to be brave when I'm with you.'

Kitty hugged him tight. She was so happy to have found Pumpkin and she was looking forward to having another adventure too!

Super facts about Cats

Super Speed

Have you ever seen a cat make a quick escape from a dog? If so, you'll know that they can move *really* fast—up to 30mph!

Super Hearing

Cats have an incredible sense of hearing and can swivel their large ears to pinpoint even the tiniest of sounds.

Super Reflexes

Have you ever heard the saying 'cats always land on their feet'? People say this because cats have amazing reflexes. If a cat is falling, they can sense quickly how to move their bodies into the right position to land safely.

Super Leaps

A cat can jump over eight feet high
in a single leap, this is due to its powerful
back leg muscles.

Super Vision

Cats have amazing night-time vision. Their
incredible ability to see in low light allows them
to hunt for prey when it's dark outside.

Super Smell

Cats have a very powerful sense of smell,
14 times stronger than a human's. Did you know
that the pattern of ridges on each cat's nose
is as unique as a human's fingerprint?

Kitty

and the
Tiger Treasure

Kitty
and the
Tiger Treasure

Girl by day. Cat by night. Ready for adventure

Written by Paula Harrison · *Illustrated by* Jenny Løvlie

Here's a taste of what's to come . . .

Kitty can't wait to visit the museum and see
the priceless Golden Tiger Statue with her own eyes.
Legend tells that those in possession of the statue can
make their greatest wish come true . . .

Kitty can't resist a little night-time adventure to
show Pumpkin the statue while there's no one else
around, but disaster strikes when the statue is stolen
and Kitty is accused of the crime.

Will Kitty clear her name, find the culprit,
and return the precious statue before sunrise?

About the author

Paula Harrison

Before launching a successful writing career,
Paula was a Primary school teacher. Her years teaching
taught her what children like in stories and how
they respond to humour and suspense. She went on
to put her experience to good use, writing many
successful stories for young readers.

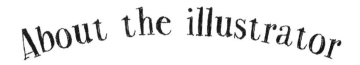

About the illustrator

Jenny Løvlie

Jenny is a Norwegian illustrator, designer,
creative, foodie, and bird enthusiast. She is fascinated
by the strong bond between humans and animals and
loves using bold colours and shapes in her work.

Love Kitty?
Why not try these too . . .